In Honor of Mossy Geer
Providence - St. Mel
Lower School Head
1993 - 1994

JosephA

FROM
MISS IDA'S
PORCH

FROM
MISS IDA'S
PORCH

by

SANDRA BELTON

illustrated by

FLOYD COOPER

FOUR WINDS PRESS ⁎ₘ⁎ *New York*
MAXWELL MACMILLAN CANADA   *Toronto*
MAXWELL MACMILLAN INTERNATIONAL   *New York   Oxford   Singapore   Sydney*

Four Winds Press
Macmillan Publishing Company
866 Third Avenue
New York, NY 10022
Maxwell Macmillan Canada, Inc.
1200 Eglinton Avenue East
Suite 200
Don Mills, Ontario M3C 3N1
Macmillan Publishing Company is part of the
Maxwell Communication Group of Companies.
First edition
Printed and bound in the United States of America.
10 9 8 7 6 5 4 3 2 1

The text of this book is set in Centaur.
The illustrations are rendered in oil wash on board.
Book design by Christy Hale

Library of Congress Cataloging-in-Publication Data
Belton, Sandra.
    From Miss Ida's porch / by Sandra Belton ; illustrated by Floyd
Cooper.—1st ed.
        p.   cm.
    Summary: In the evening the residents of Church Street gather on
Miss Ida's porch to share memories and hear stories about events in
the past, events significant to them as black people.
    ISBN 0-02-708915-0
    [1. Afro-Americans—Fiction.   2. Storytelling—Fiction.]
I. Cooper, Floyd, ill.   II. Title.
PZ7.B4197Fr   1993
[Fic]—dc20   92-31239

To the wonderful porches everywhere,
Where dreams are born and histories shared.
To the very best times that must be made for the young,
When special knowledge can be put in place
To share pride, give strength, and fasten a sense of being.
——S.B.

For my mother
——F.C.

There's a very best time of day on Church Street. My street. It begins when the sky and my feelings match, both kind of rosy around the edges.

You can hear all the best-time noises—Shoo Kate and Mr. Fisher laughing from their kitchen. Reginald and T-Bone slamming out their back door. Mr. Porter coming home from work in his noisy ole car, calling out to everybody he passes on the street. Netta practicing on her piano (mostly to get out of washing dinner dishes), and Mr. Willie making his just-checkin'-on call to Mrs. Jackson, his ninety-year-old mama.

The noises feel good.

Most of the big kids are getting ready to hang out somewhere, like at the drugstore down on the corner, or on the steps in front of the church. Those are some of their favorite pretending places—the boys pretending not to see the girls, and the girls pretending to ignore the boys. . . . Like my sister Sylvia pretending to ignore Peewee.

Most of the little kids are getting ready to get ready for bed. Getting ready for bed takes a long time for the little kids. Some of them can make it last all the way to the end of the best time. Especially the Tolver kids.

"Just five more minutes, Mama, please!" they say. Then after five minutes they hide somewhere in the yard for five more minutes. Then they start pleading all over again for five more minutes.

But most of the kids on Church Street are in-between kids. Like Freda and me.

Some of the best times we just sit on her porch or mine, playing jacks or reading comics. Sometimes we play statues with Rosetta and Punkin and Rodney. Sometimes T-Bone plays, too.

Most of the best times, though, just about all of us end up at Miss Ida's. Sitting on her porch.

Miss Ida's house is halfway down Church Street. That's probably one reason folks end up there a lot. Another reason is Miss Ida herself. She and the best time are kind of alike. Soft, peaceful.

But the biggest reason we all end up there is that Miss Ida's porch is a telling place.

Usually Mr. Fisher comes over to sit on the porch about the same time we do. It's about the time the sky is getting rosy all over. You know then that the best time is settling in.

Miss Ida calls Mr. Fisher "Poissant" because they both come from Louisiana, and that's what people there used to call him.

Mr. Fisher has been all over. It's hard to tell how old he is. But from all the stuff he's done, he could be really old. He doesn't look old at all, though. Especially when he walks. He sorta bounces. Miss Ida always says, "Poissant has a jaunty step."

Mr. Fisher has lots of memories about the places he's been and things he's seen. Almost *anything* can make him think about something he saw or heard or did a while back. He'll start out, "Puts my mind on the time . . . ," and we know what's coming.

"Tell us about that time, Poissant," Miss Ida will say to Mr. Fisher when he begins his remembering.

And he will.

Like the time Freda and Punkin were arguing about what Mrs. Jackson had said when she was over at Punkin's house, visiting Miss Esther, Punkin's aunt.

"Lena Horne ain't never visited Miz Jackson, Punkin," Freda said. "Miz Jackson was just talking outta her head, girl. You know she ninety years old. You crazy for believing her."

"You don't know nothing, Freda." Punkin was getting angry. "Just 'cause Miz Jackson's ninety don't mean she talking outta her head. Most time Miz Jackson make more sense than you!"

Punkin and T-Bone almost fell over laughing. Me, too. And this made Freda fighting mad.

"Hold on there, Miss Lady," said Mr. Fisher, taking hold of one of Freda's hands. "Don't press ugly on that pretty face. Tell me now, how come you think Lena Horne couldn't have stayed at Mrs. Jackson's house?"

"'Cause Lena Horne is famous. Why would she want to stay at Miz Jackson's?"

"Why not?" Mr. Fisher settled back in his chair.

I had a feeling that some remembering was getting started.

Used to be that most all the famous black folks who came to town stayed at somebody's house."

"How come, Mr. Fisher?" Freda sat on the stoop in front of Mr. Fisher.

"Nowhere else for them to stay! Couldn't stay in hotels. Hotels didn't allow no black guests! Famous or not. When our folk came to town to give a speech, put on a show, or whatever they came to do, we had to be the ones to give 'em a bed.

"Puts my mind on a time back in thirty-nine. I was working in West Virginia then. Working in the mines. Lived in a nice town close to where I worked. Lots of good folks there, working hard to make a life for themselves and their children."

Mr. Fisher's remembering was making him smile.

"Anyhow, a big dance took place in the town every year. Folks came from all around to go to this dance. That year, 1939, the dance was *really* going to be special. Duke Ellington was coming to town. The great bandsman himself was coming to play for the dance."

"Was Duke Ellington famous?" I bet none of us knew who Duke Ellington was. Punkin was brave enough to ask.

Mr. Fisher almost jumped out of his chair. "Don't they teach you children nothin' in school? Duke Ellington *famous*?" Mr. Fisher was almost shouting.

"Don't get bothered now, Poissant." Miss Ida put her hand on Mr. Fisher's arm. She was speaking in that peaceful way she has.

"Can't expect anybody to listen if you shouting, now can you," said Miss Ida. "Just tell the children about Duke Ellington. Tell them about the sound of that band. A sound that made your feet get a life of their own on a dance floor. Tell them how he not only led the band from his piano but also wrote most of the songs they played. How you could hum your little baby to sleep with some of those pretty songs. And how some of those songs were played by big orchestras and sung by huge choirs in halls all over the world."

Mr. Fisher had a big smile on his face. "I ain't got to tell them, Miss Ida. You doin' a fine job, a mighty fine job!"

The sky was starting to look like the never-tell blue blanket on Big Mama's bed. "Never-tell blue is light enough to still be blue but dark enough to hide the dirt," Big Mama says.

The best-time noises were still there, but they had changed. You could hear the chirping bugs. One of the Tolver kids was crying. Probably asking for something he couldn't have. Mr. Willie was playing his radio. Jazz.

Mr. Fisher was still remembering.

"Yessir. The great Duke Ellington was coming to play for us, for our dance, and there was not one hotel in the state that would put him up and take his money for doin' it. If he had a mind to rest himself in a bed, it was goin' have to be in the home of some black person."

"Did he stay with you, Mr. Fisher?" Punkin asked.

"Not with me, exactly, but in the house where I was living. Mrs. Lomax's house. Mrs. Lomax had a big, fine house, and she kept it real nice. I rented a room on the third floor."

Mr. Fisher started to grin. Like he always did when he got to a part he liked to tell.

"I was there when the great man arrived with three of his bandsmen."

"So you got to meet Duke Ellington?" T-Bone was impressed. We all were.

"I not only met him, I was there when he sat at the piano in Mrs. Lomax's parlor. Duke's playing heated up that little room. I'm telling you it did. He was some kinda good!"

Mr. Fisher grew quiet. A remembering quiet. He stopped smiling, too.

"Humph. Imagine that. A man like that. Talented, famous, everything! Not being able to pay his *own* money to sleep in a crummy little hotel room, just because he was black."

After that we were all quiet. I was wishing I knew more about what Mr. Fisher was remembering. I bet Freda was wishing so, too.

venin', everybody. Must be some powerful thinking over here tonight, 'cause everybody's deep into it."

Shoo Kate was climbing the steps to the porch. I hadn't even heard her coming up the walk. Nobody else must have either.

"Hey, Shoo Kate. Come over here by me." Miss Ida patted the place on the swing beside her.

Shoo Kate is Mr. Fisher's wife. Her name is really Mrs. Kate Fisher, but just about everybody calls her Shoo Kate. She told us one time that when she was little she used to tease her baby brother, telling him that their mama said he had to call her Sugar Kate 'cause she was so sweet. The name came out Shoo Kate when her baby brother said it. Then everybody started calling her that. She even told us kids to call her Shoo Kate instead of Mrs. Fisher.

After she sat down Shoo Kate reached over and poked Mr. Fisher. "What you been telling these folks, Fisher, to make everybody so quiet?"

"I ain't been tellin' them nothing you don't already know, darlin'." Mr. Fisher and Shoo Kate smiled at each other. They always seemed to be smiling and laughing together.

"Did any famous people stay in your house, Shoo Kate?" T-Bone asked.

"Now I know what talking's been over here," Shoo Kate said, laughing. "Fisher, you been telling them about that time Duke Ellington came and stayed at the place in West Virginia where you were living."

"I sure was," said Mr. Fisher. "No reason to keep that fine bit of history a secret."

"So it's history now, is it, Poissant," said Miss Ida. I think she was teasing. All the grown-ups laughed.

"Well, T," said Shoo Kate, "I never made history like Fisher here, but I *was* somewhere one time when history was being made."

"Shoo Kate, I bet I know what you're talking about. Go on, tell the children." Miss Ida sounded excited.

The sky was really getting dark. I like the best time most of all when the sky is dark. You can imagine that almost anything is out there. You can imagine almost anything.

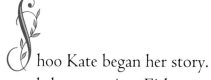

hoo Kate began her story.

"Around the same time Fisher was living in West Virginia, I was living with my family in Washington, D.C. My papa worked for the railroad. He was a train-car porter, so he had to travel most of the time. All of us looked forward to Papa's days off, the days he was going to be home.

"Oh, those were the best days—the days when Papa was home. He made sure we all did something special on those days. All of us together, Papa, Mama, and each one of us kids. We didn't have much money, but we had enough. And as shut out as we were in Washington, we could still find lots of things to do."

"What do you mean 'shut out,' Shoo Kate?" Freda asked.

"Just what the words say, sugar. Black folks were shut out. We couldn't go to the movie theaters, the big restaurants, just about anyplace you think folks ought to be able to go if the place is open to the public and folks have the inclination to go. Why, when my papa was growing up in Washington, black folks couldn't even go to the national monuments!"

Punkin looked at Shoo Kate kind of funny. "But Washington is the capital city," she said. "That's where they make laws for the whole country. How could they break the law, keeping folks from going places just 'cause they was black?"

Freda had been waiting all evening to get back at Punkin, and her chance had finally come.

"Now look who's talking outta her head! Girl, don't you know nothing? Used to be that the *law* said it was okay to keep black folks out," she said.

"Don't you two get started now. Freda's right about the laws, of course," Miss Ida said, pulling Punkin down to sit beside her. "But that's another story. A long story for another time. Go on, Shoo Kate, please."

❧

Shoo Kate did.

"Anyhow, this one time we were all real excited because Papa was going to be home for Easter. He wasn't always able to be there for holidays. So we were all looking forward to having him home and being able to dress up in our new clothes and go to church together.

"But it wasn't Papa's plan for us to go to church that Easter Sunday. After we were all dressed and ready to leave the house, Papa said we were going to catch the trolley car.

"Then we really got excited. Catching the trolley car! We knew that Papa must be planning something special because we didn't need to catch the trolley to go to our church. We only had to walk a couple of blocks to get there."

Shoo Kate sat up straighter. It was like her remembering was pushing at her back.

"How grand we were, riding on the trolley that Easter Sunday morning. And even grander when Papa explained that we were on our way to the Lincoln Memorial. That was exciting enough. Then he went on to tell us that we were going there to hear one of the greatest voices in America!"

"Who were you going to hear, Shoo Kate?" Freda asked the question this time.

"We were going to hear Marian Anderson. A grand, grand singer—a voice more magnificent than you could *ever* imagine!

"But there was more to it than just going to hear Marian Anderson sing. Much more."

Shoo Kate wiggled down to the edge of her chair and moved her face closer to us.

"It was like this. Several months before that Easter Sunday, a concert had been arranged. It was arranged for Marian Anderson to sing at Constitution Hall. Constitution Hall was the big concert stage in Washington, where all the famous musicians appeared. People from all over the world.

"Marian Anderson was certainly famous. *And* she had sung all over the world. Didn't matter, though. Marian Anderson's concert was not going to take place in Constitution Hall. You see, Marian Anderson was black. The people who owned the hall said no black musician was going to perform on their stage!"

Shoo Kate sat back in her chair. Her eyes got narrow.

"While we rode on the trolley, Papa told us what had happened. A lot of people in Washington were furious about Miss Anderson not being able to sing at Constitution Hall. The wife of the president of the United States was one of these furious people. So she and some of the others got together to arrange for Miss Anderson to sing somewhere else."

Shoo Kate starting moving her hands as she talked. Her smile started coming back.

"Constitution Hall with its white columns and high-up ceiling wouldn't welcome Marian Anderson. But the Lincoln Memorial would! There would be no walls to keep people out. And the sky would be the ceiling! On Easter Sunday morning just about anybody who wanted to would be able to hear and *see* Marian Anderson sing. Including my entire family!"

Shoo Kate's smile was all over her face.

"At first we thought it might rain. We had gotten there early, very early, hoping to get close enough to see. While we waited, we kept looking up at the sky, wishing for the sun to come out.

"The crowd grew and grew. So many people, all kinds of people. Black folks, white folks, standing there together in front of the Lincoln Memorial, waiting to hear Marian Anderson sing."

Mr. Fisher started grinning himself. What Shoo Kate was about to say must have been his favorite part of the story.

"It was about time for the concert to start. Then, just as Marian Anderson was getting ready to walk out onto the place she was gonna sing from, the sun came out. Yes, it did!"

Shoo Kate's voice grew softer. So soft we moved closer to hear her.

"When the concert started, our papa took turns holding the little ones up so they could get a better look. When he reached down to get my baby brother Jimmy, I saw tears rolling down his cheeks.

"I asked my mama if Papa was crying 'cause he was happy. This is what Mama said to us sometimes when we caught her crying. Mama said that some of Papa's tears were happy tears, but some were not. Some were tears of sadness, and maybe even anger.

"Mama said to me, 'Listen to the words she sings, Kate.' Miss Anderson was singing a song I knew, 'My Country, 'Tis of Thee.' I recognized the words:

'. . . *From every mountainside*
Let freedom ring'

" 'Your papa's thinking about those words and what they should mean,' Mama said. 'Thoughts like that might be making him feel good and bad at the same time. That's probably why there are tears on your papa's face.' "

Shoo Kate sat back in her chair. Her voice got almost regular.

"So you see, on that Easter Sunday I saw history being made there at the Lincoln Memorial. I also saw my papa cry with pride and sadness at the same time. It was a day that will live in my memory forever."

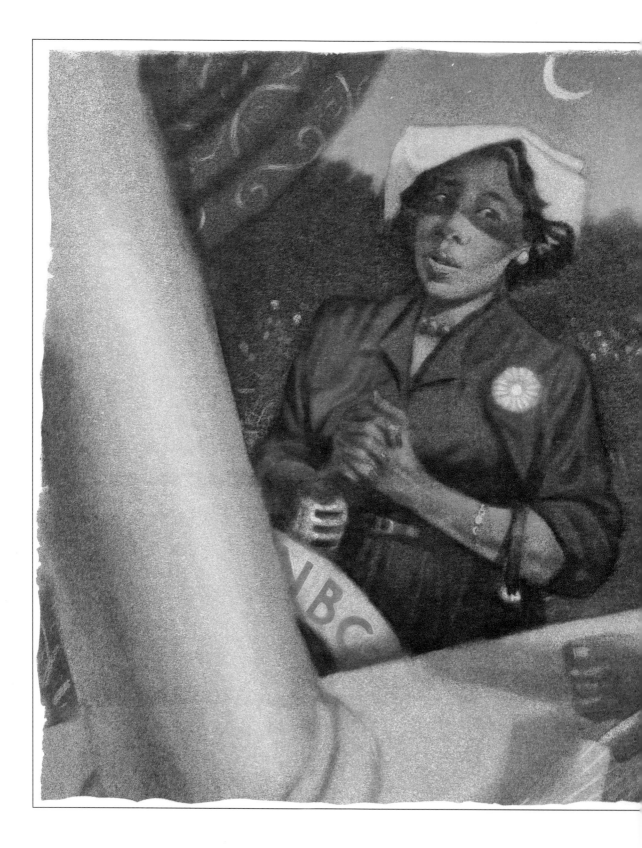

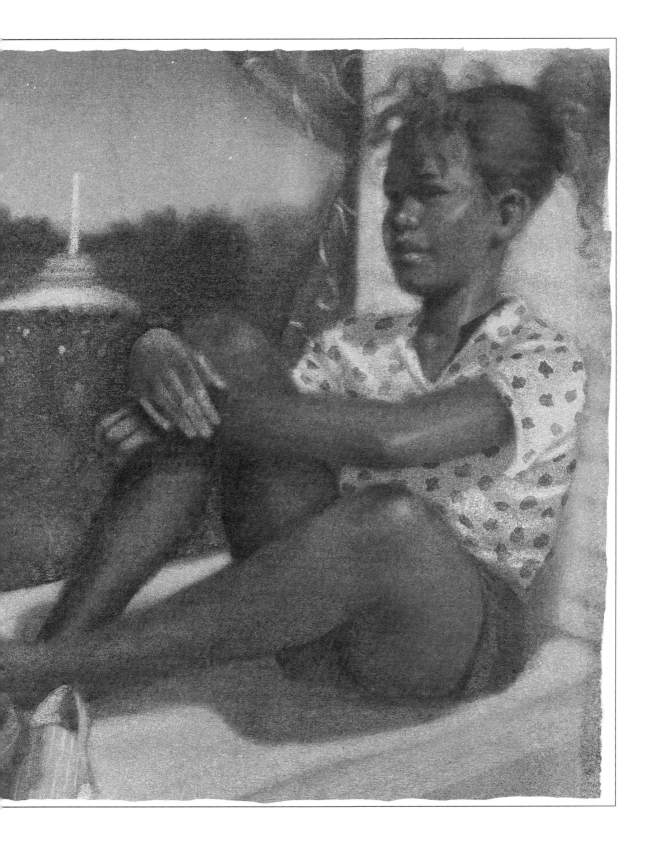

Shoo Kate's remembering had kind of put a spell on us. On everybody listening. Even Punkin was real still, and she was usually moving around like a doll on strings. When my father and my sister Sylvia walked up on the porch, we all jumped. Nobody had heard them coming.

"Goodness, you all gave me a fright." Miss Ida got up. "Hi, Sylvia. Here, take my seat, J.S.," she said to Daddy. "I'll get more chairs from the house."

"No need, Ida," Daddy said. "A few folks are going to be leaving very soon and there'll be plenty of room."

Daddy looked over at me and Freda. I knew that the very best time was about to be over for us.

"Hey, J.S., what you been up to?" Daddy and Mr. Fisher were shaking hands.

"I just been walking down to the corner to make sure Sylvia and her friends know it's time to come home."

"Sylvia don't know nothing when Peewee's around." I just had to say that. My sister thinks she's something special just 'cause bony ole Peewee said she was cute.

"Shut up!" Sylvia wanted to hit me. I just knew it.

"Don't speak that way to your sister," Daddy said to Sylvia. "And you, missy," he said pointing to me, "if you want to get your extra few minutes here, I think you'd better have kinder thoughts for Sylvia."

"There's been some wonderful thoughts on this porch tonight, folks. Let's keep the good words going." Miss Ida always makes things okay.

"J.S.," she said, "you missed a wonderful story. Shoo Kate was telling us about the time she saw Marian Anderson."

"Oh, yeah," Daddy said, like he was remembering something. "You told me a little about that, Shoo Kate. I wish I had been here to hear the whole story."

"Tell him the story, Shoo Kate. We'd love to hear it again. Right, Freda?" I wanted so much to make the best time last.

"Good try, baby, but it won't work tonight." Daddy hardly ever let my tricks work on him.

"I have another chapter for that story, however. Want to hear it?" While he was talking, Daddy winked at Shoo Kate. I thought he was fooling.

Miss Ida sat up in her seat. Like she felt the same as me. Wanting the evening to go on.

"Come on, J.S., sit down and take your turn this evening." Miss Ida motioned for us to make room for Daddy.

Then my daddy started his remembering.

I had an uncle—Uncle Henry—who lived in Washington," Daddy began. "He taught at Howard University there, for many years.

"Uncle Henry was a big man, well over six feet tall. He had wide, full eyebrows that came together like a hairy *V* whenever he frowned. And Uncle Henry frowned easily. Especially when one of us was messin' up. His voice was like a drum—booming, deep. His voice, his frown, and his attitude could put the fear of God in you. Uncle Henry didn't play!"

Daddy chuckled.

"I dearly loved Uncle Henry, though. We all did. In fact, he was probably the favorite of everybody in the family. Whenever there was going to be a family gathering, we all wanted it to be at Uncle Henry's. At Uncle Henry's you knew that there would be lots to do, lots to eat, and best of all, lots and lots of Uncle Henry."

Daddy has a deep voice, too. A good telling voice.

"Uncle Henry had worked hard to get where he wanted to be in life. And he was one of the lucky ones: He got there. Yep, Uncle Henry was a grand old guy. One of those people you hope will go on forever."

Daddy looked out into the darkness. I think he was seeing Uncle Henry in his mind. I think I was, too.

"Whenever us nephews and nieces were gathered around the breakfast or dinner table, Uncle Henry would claim the floor, but we didn't mind at all. Uncle Henry was a magnificent storyteller! And though we didn't know it then, his stories were like fuel for our young minds.

"Uncle Henry firmly believed that the knowledge of our history— the history of black folks—was the most important story that we could ever be told. I can just hear him now: 'You can know where you are going in this world only if you know where you've been!'"

Mr. Fisher slapped his hand on his leg. "Now that's a man after my own heart!" he said.

"*Shhhhh*, Fisher. Let J.S. go on," Shoo Kate said.

Daddy did. "Uncle Henry held us spellbound with his stories. He told us about the great civilizations of Africa that existed thousands of years ago, and—"

"Tell us about that!" T-Bone moved real close to Daddy.

"That's a story for another time, T," Daddy said. "I'll be sure to tell you, but I'd better get on with this one now.

"One of Uncle Henry's stories described how he had been there that Easter Sunday at the Lincoln Memorial. But that same story had another part, a part that told something that had happened *before* that famous Sunday.

"You see, another important event had taken place in that same spot seventeen years earlier—the dedication of the Lincoln Memorial. Uncle Henry had been there then, too."

"Wow!" said T-Bone and Punkin. I knew how they felt.

"It wasn't as much of a 'wow' as you might think, kids. At the dedication of this monument to the man known as the Great Emancipator, the blacks folks who came had to stand in a special section. A section off to the left of the monument. Away from the white folks, who could stand dead center, right in front."

Daddy had started breathing hard. It sounded loud. Everything else was quiet. Except Daddy's breathing.

"Anyhow, during one of our visits to Uncle Henry, Marian

Anderson was going to be giving another concert. It was very important to Uncle Henry that all the nieces and nephews have a chance to go."

"So, you heard a concert at the Lincoln Memorial, too, right?" T-Bone sure was making it hard for Daddy to get on with his story. I wanted to put some tape over his mouth.

Daddy smiled. "No, as a matter of fact, I didn't. The concert I went to was held at Constitution Hall."

"What?" All of us were surprised at this twist.

"That's right," Daddy said. His breathing wasn't so loud now. "It was 1965, over twenty-five years since that concert at the Lincoln Memorial. Marian Anderson was now at the end of her career as a singer. This concert was taking place so she could say farewell to Washington audiences.

"Constitution Hall was still one of the finest concert stages in Washington, a stage now open to all performers, no matter what their color. It had been that way for years. But that concert and that magnificent singer were special. Very special."

Everybody was looking at Daddy as he went on.

"Many of the people in the hall that night were African Americans. Some of these black people had also been standing on the grass under the sky that Easter Sunday morning. And some, like Uncle Henry, had been out there on the grass for the dedication in 1922. Now these same people were sitting in the forbidden hall, some of them in the best seats in the house!

"When Marian Anderson came onto the stage, the applause of the crowd was like the roar of a thousand pounding seas. It went on and on and on. But above the noise, there was one thing I heard very clearly."

"You heard your Uncle Henry, right?" Miss Ida was smiling at Dad. And her eyes were sparkly. Like raindrops are sparkly when I can look through them on my window and see the sun.

My dad's voice was real soft. "I did, Ida. I could hear Uncle Henry. But I think I would have known what he was saying even if I hadn't heard him. Just like I can hear him right now: 'You can know where you are going in this world only if you know where you've been!'"

In the quiet after Daddy stopped talking, I looked out into the velvet black sky. I tried to imagine the sound of a thousand pounding seas. I tried to imagine some other things, too. Like how it might have been to ride on a trolley. Or to spend the night in the same house with a famous person. Or to go to a famous monument and not be able to stand where I wanted to.

My dad's story brought the end to the very best time that evening.

Like we always did, Freda, T, Punkin, and I said good-night to all the grown-ups and walked each other home. I walked Freda home and then she walked me home, and then I walked her home again. Sylvia told on us like she usually does, so I finally went home for good to go to bed.

Just before I go to sleep is the very, very last part of the very best time. After I'm in bed and my light is turned off, I can look out my bedroom window and see Miss Ida's porch.

Most of the time the grown-ups are still there. I can hear them talking and laughing, but it's soft and far away.

These sounds feel good. They keep the very best times close. So close that they're with me when my eyelids stop cooperating and just drop. I think the very best times go with me into my dreams. . . .

A NOTE FROM THE AUTHOR

Porches are wonderful places for sharing things. So are kitchens and dinner tables and floors in front of fireplaces. Because of these places, we are introduced to many people and come to know them through stories told to us about them. But sometimes the people we hear about have such special gifts that we need to do more than imagine what it would be like to see or hear them.

Marian Anderson and Duke Ellington are two such people. It would be nearly impossible to imagine the greatness of their gifts. The following is a short list of recommended books and recordings. These other wonderful sharing places, like front porches, help great things live on.

BOOKS

Anderson, Marian. *My Lord, What a Morning: An Autobiography.* New York: Watts, 1956 (312 pp.).

*Collier, James Lincoln. *Duke Ellington.* New York: Macmillan, 1991 (144 pp., recommended for ages 10 and older).

Dance, Stanley. *The World of Duke Ellington.* New York: Da Capo Press, 1980 (311 pp.).

Gutman, Bill. *Duke.* New York: Random House, 1977 (184 pp., recommended for ages 12 and older).

*Montgomery, Elizabeth Rider. *Duke Ellington: King of Jazz.* Champaign, Ill.: Garrard, 1972 (96 pp., illustrated, recommended for ages 8 and older).

Patterson, Charles. *Marian Anderson.* New York: Watts, 1988 (160 pp., recommended for ages 12 and older).

*Tedards, Anne. *Marian Anderson.* New York: Chelsea House, 1988 (111 pp., recommended for ages 10 and older).

Vehanen, Kosti. *Marian Anderson, a Portrait.* Westport, Conn.: Greenwood Press, 1970 (270 pp.).

SOUND RECORDINGS

Marian Anderson. Pearl Gemm CD 9318 (compact disc, 1988).

Marian Anderson. RCA Victor Vocal Series. BMG Classics (compact disc, 1989).

Black, Brown, and Beige. Performed by Duke Ellington. Columbia JCS-8015 (LP, 1973).

Digital Duke. Performed by Duke Ellington. GRP Records GRD-9548 (compact disc, 1987).

Ellington Is Forever. Fantasy F79005, 79008 (LP, 1975).

Spirituals. Performed by Marian Anderson. RCA Red Seal LM 2032 (LP, 1956).

The Music of Duke Ellington Played by Duke Ellington. Columbia Special Products JCL 558 (LP, 1973).

Verdi, Giuseppe. *Un Ballo in Maschera: Highlights.* Performed by Marian Anderson. RCA VL 42831 (LP, 1979).

VIDEOTAPE RECORDINGS

Marian Anderson. The life of the legendary singer is recounted, from her early appearances in Philadelphia to concerts throughout America and Europe. Narrated by Avery Brooks. Washington, D.C.: WETA, 1991 (60 min., close-captioned).

Duke Ellington and His Orchestra. Vitaphone, 1986 (40 min., black-and-white).

Asterisks indicate material especially accessible to younger readers.
Additional resources are available at libraries, video stores, and bookstores.

SANDRA BELTON

grew up in Beckley, West Virginia, a town of wonderful porches. She lives with her family in Chicago, Illinois. This is her first book for children.

FLOYD COOPER

remembers gathering with his friends to listen to stories on Miss Martin's porch. The paintings in this book were inspired by those memories and by the Muskogee, Oklahoma, neighborhood where Floyd grew up.

The artist has illustrated several acclaimed books for children, including the ALA Notable Book *Chita's Christmas Tree* by Elizabeth Fitzgerald Howard.

Floyd Cooper lives in Parlin, New Jersey.